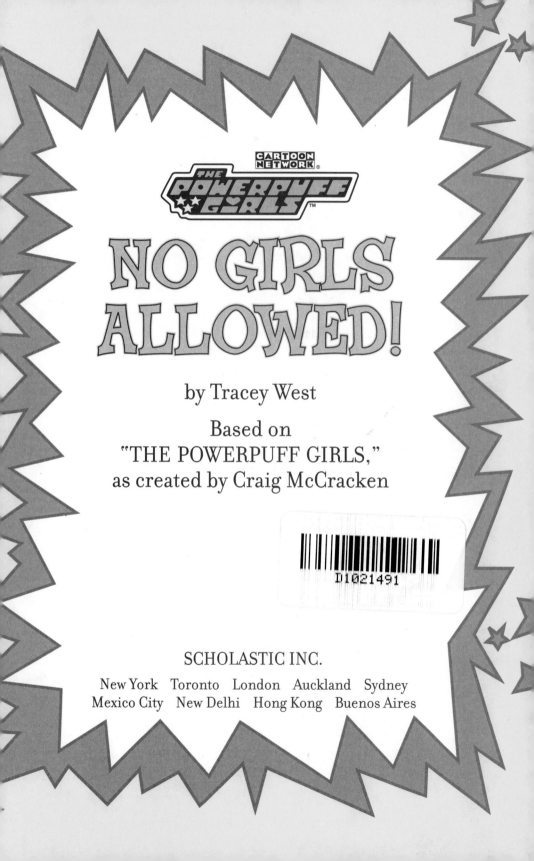

CARTOON NETWORK®

THE POWERPUFF GIRLS™

NO GIRLS ALLOWED!

by Tracey West

Based on
"THE POWERPUFF GIRLS,"
as created by Craig McCracken

D1021491

SCHOLASTIC INC.

New York   Toronto   London   Auckland   Sydney
Mexico City   New Delhi   Hong Kong   Buenos Aires

ISBN 0-439-29588-2

Designed by Peter Koblish
Illustrated by Cindy Morrow

12 11 10 9 8 7 6 5 4 3 2 1   1 2 3 4 5 6/0

Printed in the U.S.A.

First Scholastic printing, September 2001

The city of Townsville, where happy people laugh and play in the park.

But not everybody was happy today. The Powerpuff Girls saw that the girls of Townsville looked very upset.

"Something is wrong," said Blossom.

"Maybe we can help," said Bubbles.

"Maybe we can pound someone for them!" said Buttercup.

"Girls, why are you so sad?" Bubbles asked.

Julie Bean pointed. "Some boys have made a clubhouse," she said. "A clubhouse just for boys!"

The Powerpuff Girls read the sign. It said, NO GIRLZ ALLOWED!

"'No girls allowed' is no fair," said Julie Bean. "We want to go inside the clubhouse. Can you help us?"

Blossom stopped her sister.

"We do not have to fight the boys," she said. "We can talk to them."

Blossom zoomed to the clubhouse. She knocked on the door.

"Hey, boys, let us in," Blossom said. "There is room in the clubhouse for boys *and* girls."

A loud voice boomed through the door. "No girls allowed!"

Bubbles had an idea.

"Maybe we can ask them nicely," she said.

Bubbles zoomed to the clubhouse. She knocked on the door.

"Pretty please, may we come in?" Bubbles asked.

The loud voice boomed again.

"NO GIRLS ALLOWED!"

Buttercup tried next. She zoomed to the clubhouse. She pounded on the door. "Let us in right now!" she yelled.

"*Now* can we pound our way in?" asked Buttercup.

"You bet!" said Blossom and Bubbles.

The Powerpuff Girls zoomed back to the clubhouse. They blasted a hole in the wall.

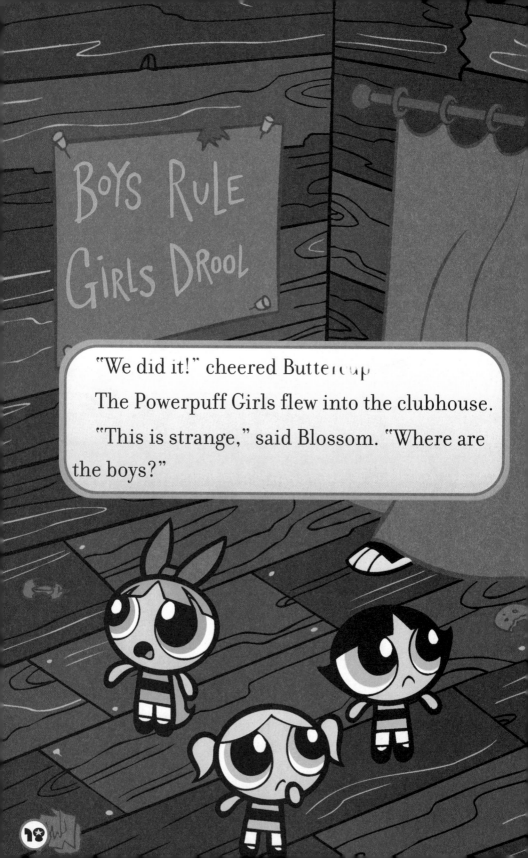

"We did it!" cheered Buttercup.

The Powerpuff Girls flew into the clubhouse.

"This is strange," said Blossom. "Where are the boys?"

Slam! A cage dropped down.

"Oh, no!" wailed Bubbles. "We are trapped!"

Five boys stepped into the room.

"The Gangreen Gang!" Blossom cried. "I should have known you bullies were behind this."

Ace, the leader, laughed. "We knew you would try to get into our clubhouse. We wanted to get you out of our way."

"Yesssssss," hissed Snake.

"Now we can have some fun with the kids in the park," said Ace.

"We will eat their food," said Little Arturo.

"We will kick ssssand in their facessss," said Snake.

"Let's go, boys!" Ace yelled.

"Ace's idea of fun is no fun at all," said Bubbles. "We have to get out of here."

"That is easy," said Buttercup. "We can blast through these bars with our eye beams."

"We may be too late," said Blossom. "Who knows what kind of trouble the Gangreen Gang will make?"

Outside, the Gangreen Gang was ready for action. "The Powerpuff Girls are trapped," said Ace. "Now we can spoil everyone's happy day at the park. Let's go make some babies cry."

"What did you do to The Powerpuff Girls?" asked Julie Bean.

"Out of our way, girlie," said Ace. "We have work to do."

"You will have to get through us first," said Julie. "Get them, girls!"

The girls kept the Gangreen Gang busy. Soon Blossom, Bubbles, and Buttercup were free.

"Thanks, girls," said Blossom. "We will take it from here."

Bing! Bang! Boom! In a flash, The Powerpuff Girls had trapped the Gangreen Gang.

"Hooray!" cheered the girls of Townsville. "Now the clubhouse is ours."

"That is right," said Buttercup. "Now the rule is no BOYS allowed."

"That will make *us* happy," said Bubbles. "But I have an idea that will make *everybody* happy."

"Everybody but the Gangreen Gang," added Blossom.

So once again, the day is saved . . . thanks to The Powerpuff Girls and the girls of Townsville!